CW00864049

About the Author

Sue Lawrence loved her cat Harry who gave her the inspiration to write stories about him. Sue lived in London with her son, Asten and would use her imagination to allow Harry to go on his adventures and meet new friends. Recently Sue has moved to the Hampshire countryside where she continues to write about Harry and his adventures.

Dedication

I would like to dedicate this book to my son Asten and my mum, Bronwen, for believing in me.

Sue Lawrence

HARRY

AUSTIN MACAULEY
PUBLISHERS LTD.

Copyright © Sue Lawrence (2017)

The right of Sue Lawrence to be identified as author of this work has been asserted by her in accordance with section 77 and 78 of the Copyright, Designs and Patents Act 1988.

All rights reserved. No part of this publication may be reproduced, stored in a retrieval system, or transmitted in any form or by any means, electronic, mechanical, photocopying, recording, or otherwise, without the prior permission of the publishers.

Any person who commits any unauthorised act in relation to this publication may be liable to criminal prosecution and civil claims for damages.

A CIP catalogue record for this title is available from the British Library.

ISBN 9781787102101 (Paperback)
ISBN 9781787102118 (E-Book)

www.austinmacauley.com

First Published (2017)
Austin Macauley Publishers Ltd.
25 Canada Square
Canary Wharf
London
E14 5LQ

Happy Christmas Penny

Lots of Love

and xxxxx's

From

Nanny Jan and Grandad Rog.

xxx
x

2019

Harry is a friendly, rather large, Tabby cat who's just moved into Eighty Nine Pavilion Way.

Harry spends most of his days looking out of the kitchen window as he cannot go out on his own for a few weeks yet until he finds his bearings.

He lives there with his brother and his mum who adopted him when he was just a kitten.

Harry, like most cats, loves to lie about and do nothing. His favourite place is stretched out on the sofa when his owners are out and he can shut his eyes for a while.

Suddenly Harry found himself out in the garden of Eighty Nine and someone from over the fence was calling him.

Harry got up and peeped over the fence. There standing in the middle of the pond, wearing a rather long pair of wellie boots, was a long legged bird.

"Hello," he said, "I'm Long Legs, you must be the new guy that everyone is talking about, the one who is taken for walks on a lead," and with that burst out laughing.

"We first thought you were a funny looking dog," he said. Harry nearly died of embarrassment! "Anyway mate," he said, "nice to meet you at last."

Harry introduced himself and asked him what he was doing standing in the middle of a pond up to his neck in water.

Long Legs replied, "watch and learn," and with that Long Legs placed his head under the water and pulled out one of Mr Pringles's Koi Carp.

Harry couldn't believe his eyes, it was the biggest fish he had ever seen. Mr Pringles is Harry's next door neighbour at Eighty Seven, he's a grumpy old man who never stops moaning.

Long Legs calls round at Eighty Seven every morning to catch his breakfast but must wait until Mr Pringles goes for his morning papers.

Harry spent hours chatting and watching Long Legs pull out the fish one by one. As he watched, Harry thought how easy it looked, he crept up to the edge of the pond and took a closer look.

There sitting on a lily pad staring at him was a funny looking creature that Harry had never seen before. He was a green, slimy-looking fella and he was holding a fishing rod in one hand and in the other a net. Next to him was a tiny picnic basket full of worms and he was eating one of Harry's favourite dishes, flies!

"Afternoon Harry," he said, "I'm Rebbit." Harry's stomach began to rumble and his mouth started to water, he crept up, his tail started wagging and he was just about to pounce when he lost his footing. All of a sudden Harry slipped off the edge of the rockery!

Harry shut his eyes tight, when he opened them he saw his owner looking straight at him. Harry found himself back on the sofa soaking wet!